OGDEN LRC

W9-CCC-738

It is not time for sleeping :

IT IS NOT TIME FOR SLEEPING

(A Bedtime Story)

LISA GRAFF
LAUREN CASTILLO

CLARION BOOKS
Houghton Mifflin Harcourt
Boston   New York

OGDEN AVENUE SCHOOL
501 W. OGDEN
LA GRANGE, IL 60525

Clarion Books
3 Park Avenue
New York, New York 10016

Text copyright © 2016 by Lisa Graff
Illustrations copyright © 2016 by Lauren Castillo

All rights reserved.
For information about permission to reproduce selections from this
book, write to trade.permissions@hmhco.com or to Permissions,
Houghton Mifflin Harcourt Publishing Company,
3 Park Avenue, 19th Floor, New York, New York 10016.

Clarion Books is an imprint of Houghton Mifflin Harcourt Publishing Company.

www.hmhco.com

The art was created in ink and watercolor on Arches Hot Press paper.
The text was set in 16 pt. Letterpress Text Roman.
Design by Christine Kettner

LIBRARY OF CONGRESS CATALOGING-IN-PUBLICATION DATA
Names: Graff, Lisa (Lisa Colleen), 1981– | Castillo, Lauren, illustrator.
Title: It is not time for sleeping : (a bedtime story) / Lisa Graff ; Lauren Castillo.
Description: Boston ; New York : Clarion Books, Houghton Mifflin Harcourt, [2016] |
Summary: Bedtime is near, but from the end of dinner until lights are turned off, it is not really
time for sleeping until a child receives a special good night wish.
Identifiers: LCCN 2015020441 | ISBN 9780544319301 (hardcover)
Subjects: | CYAC: Bedtime—Fiction. | Parent and child—Fiction.
Classification: LCC PZ7.G751577 It 2016 | DDC [E]—dc23
LC record available at http://lccn.loc.gov/2015020441

Manufactured in Malaysia
TWP 10 9 8 7 6 5 4 3 2 1
4500602160

To Nathan
—L.G.

For Anne, Colleen, Ronan, Jonathan,
Henry, Holly, and Matt
—L.C.

When I've munched and crunched my last three carrots
(except for one I fed to Jasper), Mom takes my plate.
"It's been a good day," she says.
"It *is* a good day," I tell her.
Because the day's not finished yet.

And it is not time for sleeping.

When dinner is over,
Dad runs water in the sink. I squeeze the soap and make bubbles.
"It's getting dark," he says, while he scrubs and scrubs.
"It could be darker," I tell him.

It is not time for sleeping.

When dinner is over and the dishes are scrubbed,
I get in my bath. Jasper tries to join me. We only splash a bit.
"Better get out soon," Mom says.
I stretch my wrinkled toes. "Just a little longer," I tell her.

It is not time for sleeping.

When dinner is over and the dishes are scrubbed and I'm squeaky-squeak clean, Mom zips up my pajamas, the bear ones with feet.

I **ROAR** at Jasper.

"Don't you look cozy!" Dad says.

I stretch my tallest stretch.
"Not *too* cozy," I tell him.

It is not time for sleeping.

When dinner is over and the dishes are scrubbed and
I'm squeaky-squeak clean and zipped up to my chin,
Dad holds me by my ankles while I brush my teeth,
top ones on bottom and bottoms on top.
"Getting tired, silly goose?" Dad asks my feet.
I yawn an upside-down yawn. "Nope," I tell him.

It is not time for sleeping.

When dinner is over and the dishes are scrubbed and
I'm squeaky-squeak clean and zipped up to my chin and
my teeth are shiny, I say good night to Jasper. He licks
both my ears.
"Yip!" he yips.

I rub him on his belly, where the fur
is fluffy soft. "Almost," I tell him.

It is not time for sleeping.

When dinner is over and the dishes are scrubbed and
I'm squeaky-squeak clean and zipped up to my chin and
my teeth are shiny and I've said good night to Jasper,
I climb into bed. Mom tucks me in with the covers
smooth and tight.

"You look ready for a good night's sleep," she says.

I blink my heavy eyes. Open, closed, open.
"Maybe soon," I tell her.

It is not time for sleeping.

When dinner is over and the dishes are scrubbed and
I'm squeaky-squeak clean and zipped up to my chin and
my teeth are shiny and I've said good night to Jasper and
I'm tucked tight in my bed, Dad reads me a story.
I snuggle down under the covers to listen.

"That was a nice one," he says when he's done.

I tug the blankets up past my nose. "Mmm," I tell him.

But it is still not time for sleeping.

When dinner is over and the dishes are scrubbed and
I'm squeaky-squeak clean and zipped up to my chin and
my teeth are shiny and I've said good night to Jasper and
I'm tucked tight in my bed and the story is done, Mom
turns off the lights. All I can see is the glow from the hall.

"It's really, truly bedtime," Mom says.

I rub my eyes. "Not yet," I tell her, very soft.
"Not until one more thing you both forgot."

Mom and Dad lean in close.

"We'd never forget," they say.
And they hug me tight.

"Good night, sweet darling," they whisper. "We love you."

I stretch out comfy in my bed. "I love you, too,"
I whisper back. "Good night." And I close my eyes.

Because now . . .

Now . . .

Now it is time . . .

for sleeping.